Kyoto-Dwelling

Kyoto-Dwelling

A YEAR OF BRIEF POEMS

by

EDITH SHIFFERT

illustrations by Kohka Saito

Charles E. Tuttle Company

RUTLAND, VERMONT & TOKYO, JAPAN

REPRESENTATIVES

British Isles & Continental Europe:
Simon & Schuster International Group, *London*

Australasia: Bookwise International
1 Jeanes Street, Beverley, 5009, South Australia

Some of the poems in this book were previously published in *Kansai Time Out, Kyoto Review, Mainichi Daily News,* and *Poetry Nippon.*

Published by the Charles E. Tuttle Company, Inc.
of Rutland, Vermont & Tokyo, Japan
with editorial offices at
Suido 1-chome, 2-6, Bunkyo-ku, Tokyo

Copyright © 1987
by Charles E. Tuttle Co., Inc.

All rights reserved

Library of Congress Catalog Card No. 87-50162
International Standard Book No. 0-8048-1528-3

First printing, 1987

Printed in Japan

*This collection of brief poems
is dedicated to
a happy old man of Kyoto*
MINORU SAWANO

TABLE OF CONTENTS

List of Illustrations	*page* 9
Introduction	11
The Poems:	
January	20
February	28
March	36
April	44
May	52
June	60
July	68
August	76
September	84
October	92
November	100
December	108

LIST OF ILLUSTRATIONS

January: *Snowy Daimonji*	20–21
February: *Plum blossoms and bush warbler*	29
March: *Buson's gravestone*	37
April: *Cherry trees in the dusk*	44–45
May: *Mountain wisteria*	53
June: *Hydrangeas in the rain*	61
July: *Water lilies and frog*	69
August: *Reedy pond and wild ducks*	76–77
September: *Tender hagi*	84–85
October: *Buson's tea hut*	93
November: *Persimmon tree and birds*	101
December: *Sparrows in the snow*	109

INTRODUCTION

Perhaps these brief poems will make a story of a daily life at the foot of Mount Hiei in Kyoto. An American woman, her Japanese husband, and the landlord's dogs.

> *Hiyo* bird calls me—
> a black cat sneaking away!
> The dogs keep sleeping.

Since I came to Kyoto in 1963, much has changed, but even more has not changed. They are the things written about here, at the moments when they were experienced.

The most important word in the title of this book is not "Kyoto" but rather "Dwelling." That means having residence at a place, a shelter where one stays for some time, the act of being and noticing from a particular place. Since all my Kyoto dwellings are written of in this presentation, I will list them.

For the first month I had a room on Yoshida-yama, a hill overlooking much of the city and covered with temples, trees, and old graveyards.

> New to Kyoto, sounds
> of temple bells at evening
> are satisfying.

Then I was able to rent several cold rooms at one end of one of the many subsidiary temples of Myoshinji at the northwest side of the city.

> Allowed to ring it,
> bell of thirteen hundred years,
> I strike—and listen.

For the next three years I was in the northeast, near Midoro-ga-ike and Takara-ga-ike, ponds surrounded by steep hills densely vegetated and with numerous birds.

> In this small garden
> tall hydrangea hedges
> sheltering sparrows.

My next home had the Kamo River on the west and Kamigamo Shrine on the east. It looked toward the north mountains, often snow covered and with winds sweeping down during typhoons and in winter.

> Now men are cutting
> an ancient tree at the shrine
> after last night's storm.

For nine years I had a little Japanese-style house on the west bank of the Takano River which flows out of areas north and east of Kyoto and near my house joins the Kamo River.

> From the river bank
> this morning too, water birds
> and eastern ridges.

For two years I lived in a new apartment house isolated in the middle of vegetable and rice fields. The latter, when flooded in summer, were beautifully loud all night with the innumerable frogs who dwelt in them. The whole area was beginning to be developed with apartments and shops after being vast farming fields without roads.

> Like a rice-pond rock,
> sleeping with thousands of frogs
> who won't keep quiet.

Since 1981 I have had a bamboo grove close on the

east side and forest on the north, their leaves almost brushing the windows. The bamboo grove has decreased a little, but because some imperial family members are in a small graveyard at its highest point, it should remain fairly undisturbed. Beyond is a forest ascending in ridges to the top of Mount Hiei, and hiking trails which can lead to there begin at our back gate. Though Mount Hiei is only 2,782 feet high, it seems much more, since it is conspicuous from any part of Kyoto and its steepness, many ridges, deep ravines, and heavy vegetation, with only a few access roads, make it seem quite remote. Deer and wild monkeys are found there, and foxes, boars, and badgers.

At the top is the temple of Enryaku, which was founded in the eighth century and was one of the most important temples in the history of Buddhism as well as the history of the Kyoto area. Wandering on the slopes of these ridges that extend along the entire east side of Kyoto, one can know the physical land that existed before there was a Japanese race or language.

Some of these poems mention persons who used to live here. The artist Tomioka Tessai about one hundred and fifty years ago resided just above my home in what used to be a temple. The Taoist hermit Hakuyu-shi lived in a nearby forest cave in the seventeenth century. Hakuin, the famed Zen reformer and reviver, meditated with him there in his youth and regarded him as a teacher.

> On this same pathway
> Hakuin and Hakuyu
> meeting each other?

The haiku poet Yosa Buson, who was also a famed eighteenth-century artist, restored a tea hut at the temple of Kompukuji, where the haiku poet he considered his master, Matsuo Basho, had met with other haiku poets in the seventeenth century. It is in walking distance of my house, and the very old priest there is also a haiku poet and a friend. Innumerable other persons of the past whose work is still appreciated wandered these same lanes and pathways and were influenced by the daily changes of Kyoto's weather and events. There are a number of good books that give details of these, as well as books that reproduce paintings and have translations of haiku and other poetry. My little poems I prefer not to specifically label haiku now, as I do them in response to daily occurrences of this place, which might be any place, and do not at present have an interest in discussing what is and isn't good haiku.

I would like to mention that I first learned of Taoism and Buddhism from Dr. Hans Nordevin von Koerber fifty years ago.

> Tao which can be told,
> not Tao. But my old teacher,
> dead, I remember.

Later I studied with his former student Dr. Vincent Shih. Since then I have had many teachers to whom I am very indebted but to whom I was never a good pupil because of my stubborn independence. Perhaps I really got my impulses from my English father who, in an early dwelling in Fairport, New York, used to take me walking beside the Erie Barge Canal and across farmers' fields to woodlands, and who taught me of the Greek philosophers, geology, and the pleasures of going for a walk.

> Peeling an apple
> found beside a dusty road,
> my father feeds me.

With my first husband, Steven Shiffert, I was able to take long back-packing trips in Washington's Cascade Mountains, in California and Alaska, to Hawaii's volcanos when there were no roads up them, and learned to do subsistence living in lonely places.

> I remember rocks
> of glaciers and volcanos
> and in my gardens.

In recent years my companion has been my husband, Minoru Sawano, who is a natural Taoist as well as a member of a Buddhist temple and the Tenrikyo Church.

> Thank you, old man,
> being a good companion
> in these small mountains.

Through the garden of this house runs a small stream with the white sand that continuously breaks off from Mount Hiei's crumbling granite. The city is more than a thousand years old and rapidly changing. But even the mountains are breaking down. The vegetation remains thick, much of it evergreen and flowering, and the autumn colors are unsurpassed. The winter coldness seems to last a long time, but then birds come from Siberia to dwell in the Kamo River, which is much warmer than their other homes. Though much changes, Kyoto remains an aesthetically and spiritually satisfying place in which to dwell.

> This love for the earth
> is all I need to survive.
> My pack sack holds much.

Too, there is the Kyoto that is nowhere in particular. A Taoist realm, a place of imagined *satori*, somewhere like anywhere in America or Europe or Asia in any century. The sound of rain. The sound of wind. The silence of falling snow. Ridges disappearing into mist. A sudden bursting out of masses of blossoms. Birds in the early morning. Eroding rocks that blow away as sand. Flowing water. And if there are sounds of temple bells and priests chanting, that might be anywhere in Asia now or long ago. This Kyoto is very actual, physical. Leaves and frogs emerge only after precise causes, in exact repeated patterns. To participate in these natural events lets one be briefly timeless and universal, one with sages of any era who saw and heard and felt the changing temperatures and occurrences of nature.

> These little mountains
> all around me day and night
> give me my shelter.
>
> How softly the cat
> walks past the sleeping dog.
> The afternoon heat.

Kyoto, Japan

THE POEMS

JANUARY

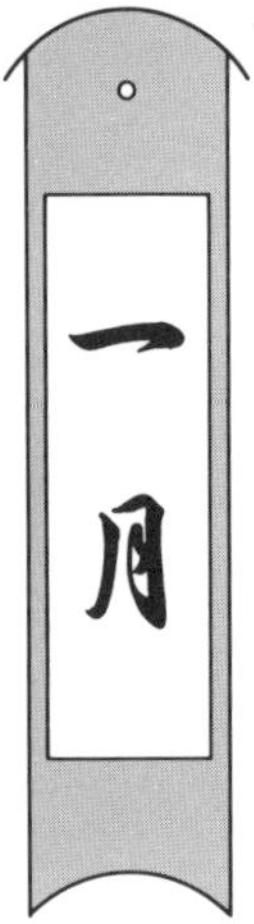

一月

*In early morning,
snowfall, and Daimonji's peak
just a white shadow.*

The faint light of dawn
makes a shining on the frost.
Lo, a year's first day.

In a cold, cold dawn
    the golden fragment of a
        waning moon—how bright!

Eleven o'clock
    and sunlight is almost warm.
    The year's first sparrows!

Each new year farther
    away from the beginning
        and nearer an end.

A happy New Year
    the old man hopes he will have.
    His bare skull glistens.

This New Year again
below Tanizaki's grave,
oh, first plum blossoms!

Inside the plum grove
    only one tree with blossoms.
        Blue, blue winter sky!

Upper half in clouds
    and the lower slopes in snow—
    Daimonji's New Year.

Above the thick snow
    covering the storehouse roof
        a persimmon branch.

Snow on the garden,
    and little birds, then larger
    birds from the mountains.

Hooked over leafless
maple twigs, fallen needles
from the taller pines.

Only a trickle
    over the rocks but louder
        than summer torrents.

Not really alone
    in mountains but pretending
    to be—like Ryokan.

Huddled, an ibis
    near a rock in the river.
        The winter day, dark.

While snow is falling
    herons wade in the river,
    their feathers all white.

 With wind the bamboos
shake off the clinging snowflakes
as soon as they come.

The mountain whitens
    and disappears in the sky.
        The roofs snowy too!

Drip, drip, the snow!
    We can hardly bear to look,
    so bright the sunshine.

Now wind blows it down—
    the snow that covered everything—
        and sunshine melts it.

I feed the sparrows
    two extra slices of bread.
    My birthday and cold.

A snowy garden
with footprints of just a cat.
Last night in the storm?

Her brown hair all wet,
    she stands out in the snowstorm—
        the tied-up old dog.

Holding a rock
    I remember high mountains
    walked on long ago.

This mountain dwelling,
    a little cold in winter
        waiting for snowfall.

I will cleanse my mind
    in this frozen waterfall
    without getting wet.

The foreign graveyard
after a long climb upward.
Snow on the forest.

Close to the oil stove
    and the sound of the kettle.
        Will the snowing stop?

An old stone lantern
    topped by a mound of new snow.
    Not a stone lantern?

Through an open door
    a curtain of falling snow,
        its motion endless.

A Japanese flute
    sounds from across a river.
    The snow keeps falling.

FEBRUARY

Petals drifting off
as a bush warbler comes down
to some plum blossoms.

February / 29

Into my silence
taking the grove of bamboo
and falling snowflakes.

When springtime is cold
    and leaves not yet appearing,
        then, the plum blossoms.

Just a few of them,
    red blossoms on the plum trees
        wet with winter rain.

A few snowflakes
    caught in plum-tree crevices,
        scent of white blossoms.

Hands cold in the wind,
    a happy old man brushes
        plum trees onto paper.

Bringing in the quilts
still warm with sunshine, shall I
take a noon-time nap?

Too dark for seeing
    and nothing that can be heard
        beyond the window.

So simple the day
    slices of toast at bedtime
    seem like a solace.

The roof keeps out rain.
    Space is warmed with an oil stove.
        Pretend its a cave.

In the winter field,
    on each uprooted turnip
    a small mound of snow.

How golden the carp
under the slightly frozen
surface of the pond.

Eternally washed,
    pebbles in the narrow stream
        of clean snow water.

Alone and silent,
    in the middle of the river
        stands a white heron.

Hurrying somewhere,
    one bird goes across the sky
        just before darkness.

Hundreds of seagulls
    back and forth over our heads,
        excited by crumbs.

The pigeons come too
and dart their beaks by the gulls'
beaks picking up crumbs.

A horde of sparrows
    hardly seen in brown grasses—
        the sound of their wings.

A pair of herons,
    the way they turn in the air
    with long legs dangling.

Close to the cold earth,
    purple berries and red ones—
        doves wait while we pass.

In the winter haze,
    how Mount Hiei hovers there
    over palace pines.

At dawn the sandals
placed by the temple steps,
their prints in new snow.

On the dark roof tiles
    white kittens with their mother.
        Snowfall in sunshine.

A field at twilight
    with a tree full of plum blossoms
    and a strolling cat.

At night a black cat
    sits and watches the tied dogs,
        enjoying their shrieks.

On a steep hillside
    being bamboo for a while
    I absorb sunshine.

Sunlight is shining
warm on my back and I sit
heedless of all else.

As they are so few,
    the plum blossoms excite us
        this cold winter day.

A complete silence
    and the first pale violets
    out of a bare cliff.

Still with cap and scarf
    my head feels the chilling wind.
        Below Mount Hiei.

Thick snow keeps falling
    on the roof of a small shrine
    and wind is blowing.

MARCH

三月

> *Spiraling toward heaven*
> *dragon pine-tree just behind*
> *Buson's gravestone.*

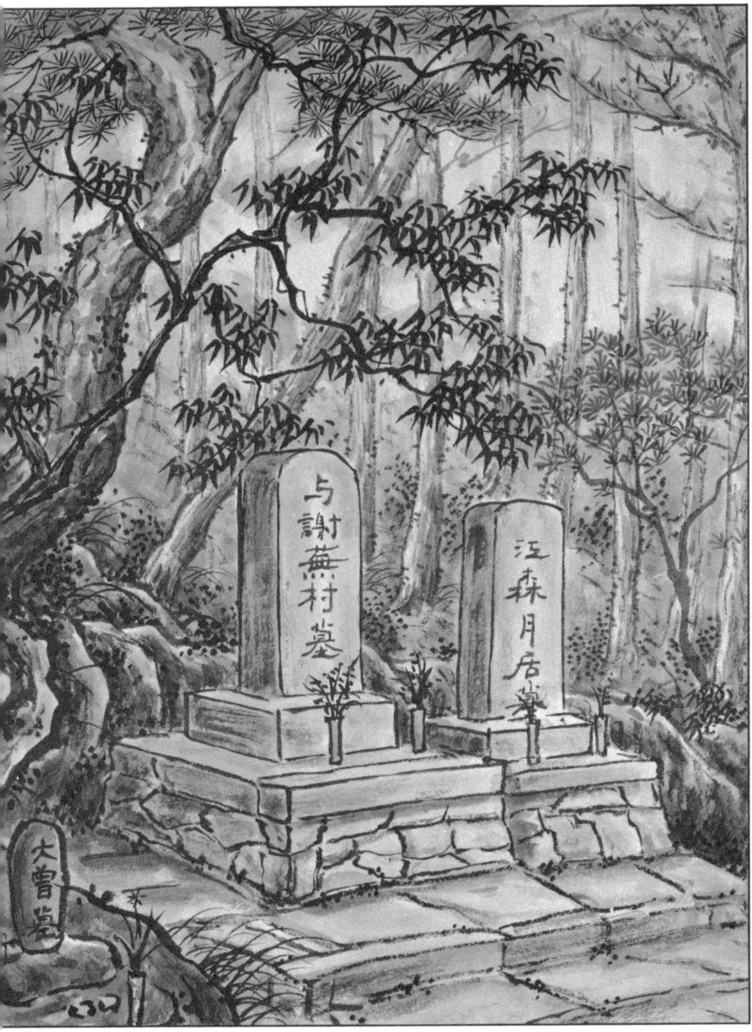
与謝蕪村墓
江森月居

Black cat beside me
on a palace-garden bench,
purring at a hand!

A thousand bamboos
    rising straight up from the earth—
        a thousand shadows!

One ray of sunlight
    deep in the bamboos, shining
        on a small Jizo.

Sheltered by the hill,
    bamboos barely move at all—
        but in the open!

Sitting for an hour
    by the tea hut without tea.
    Basho and Buson!

Each tells the other—
fisherman and woodcutter—
about the weather.

Above the wood fence
   of an abandoned old house
      a plum tree flowers.

Sounds of birds and dogs
   and the water flowing by
      my secluded house.

After all those years
   the only things that remain,
      a few brief poems.

Knowing that we wept
   but forgetting why it was,
      should we be laughing?

In the thousand arms
of the mountain, like Kannon's,
sleeping peacefully.

Treetop to treetop
    the bulbul darts in sunshine.
        That snow on the ground!

The palace plum-trees
    are full of blossoms again.
    The old Emperor!

That noble old man,
    my husband, he is laughing.
        Birds sing, and dogs bark!

A large old black cat—
    the two dogs and the old man
    watch while she strolls by.

See, the silly goose
is following the old man
dropping cracker crumbs.

Resting a moment,
    looking up at the bright sky,
        the old man too shines.

Hard to remember
    that the sky is deep in clouds
    just to the earthbound.

Breaking spider webs
    to peer over a gateway—
        broken steps inside.

This Kyoto dwelling
    reveals as many seasons
    as eternity.

This mountain shelter
when there is wind and raining
is not a shelter.

While I watch the storm
    Mozart's music in the room
        and gentle snoring.

On his single mat
    afloat in the universe
        the old man journeys.

Barking at my guests,
    the old dog looks up at me
        and wags her old tail.

The spread of mildew
    on my wall like *sumie*
        interests my guests.

The bamboo branches
caught in passing winds must dance
like helpless humans.

Listening to the rain
    all afternoon on bamboos,
        sometimes dozing off.

My finger also
    pointing at the mirrored moon
    shows on the water!

One *uguisu*
    calling from mountain forests,
        the first violet.

Each small violet
    in the deep forest, somehow,
        has turned toward the south!

APRIL

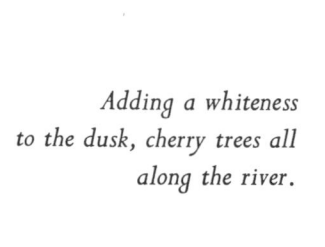

四月

*Adding a whiteness
to the dusk, cherry trees all
along the river.*

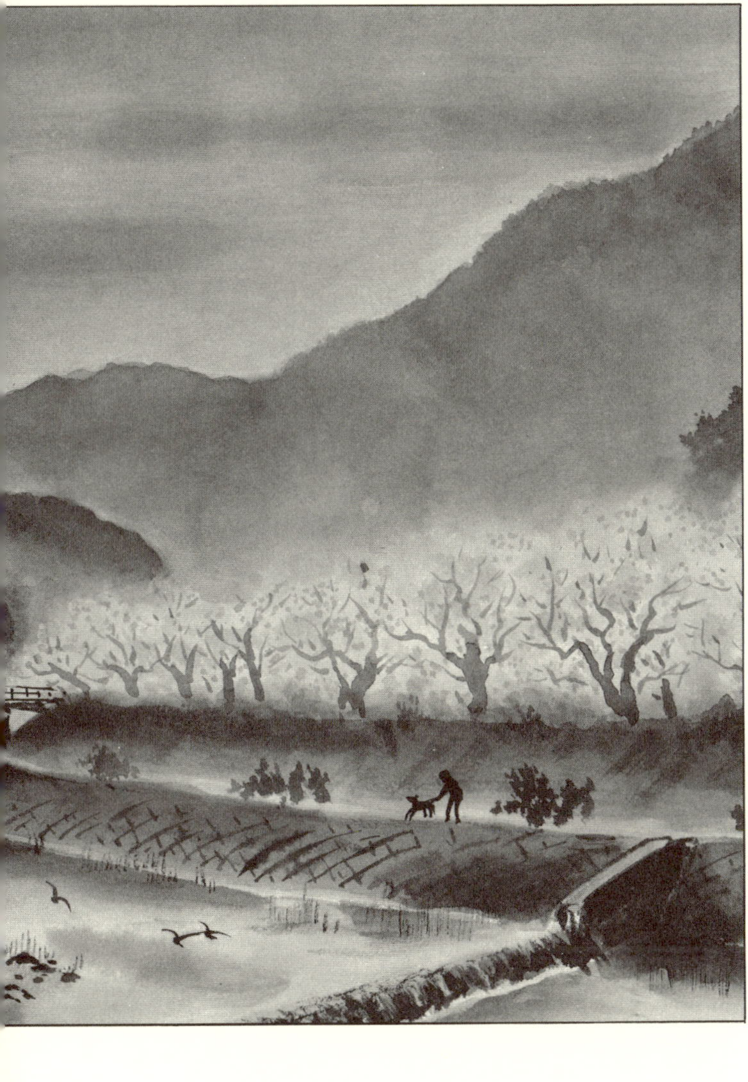

How slowly we walk
through the brightness of this spring—
hills of azaleas.

Even with new leaves
    the forest valley is dark.
        Orange azaleas!

The happy old man
    with light shining on his head
    glides down the pathway.

Tao cannot be known,
    but watch the sane old man
        treading his pathway.

In the western hills
    delicate leaves cover earth,
    small flowers by streams.

Because of the rain
the monk's tucked-up robe is stained.
Frogs in mud puddles.

Under the footsteps,
    between stones of the pavement,
        reddish violets.

As the priest gestures
    the candlelight wavers.
    Shadows are moving.

The Buddha is hidden
    past strings of brass ornaments
        in temple darkness.

Daylight with supper
    and new leaves at the window.
    Crows flying toward home.

Along the trailside
frogs within their winter holes
croaking at the spring.

From a muddy bank
    one toad voice talking, talking.
        The silent forest.

On a rain puddle
    frog eggs, and tiny tadpoles
    beginning to move.

Wet left on a rock
    where a turtle scrambles up
        out of an old pond.

A flock of small bright birds?
    No, bamboo branches suddenly
    freed by the south wind.

This morning rainfall
drips from bamboo and maple.
The hills, half hidden.

Great temples below
    are only sounds of their bells
        blown upward with winds.

At dusk a white cat
    drinking from the garden stream—
        like mine long ago.

The far temple bell
    rung on Yoshida mountain
        wakens me to spring.

Just as expected,
    violets on a sunny slope.
    The stream runs loudly.

Fallen camellias
where he waits to help me cross
the broken pathway.

Clouds in the sky
    and clouds all over hillsides
        of cherry flowers.

Today he wanders
    where cherry-blossom petals
    drift to his bald head.

In all the ditches
    drifts of pale cherry petals
        for just these few days.

As the air darkens
    they become more bright—half moon
    and cherry blossoms.

A billion petals,
each one falling separately—
along the river.

Forest of new leaves
    with azaleas' purple light
        all up the mountain.

Far in a forest,
    in front of a shrine mirror,
    two wagtails bowing.

While I look upward
    at a crow by Buson's grave
        the old priest sits near.

Now it is morning
    the birds have come to be fed.
    Last night's faded moon!

MAY

五月

*Hung from the treetops
banners of wisteria
all through the mountains.*

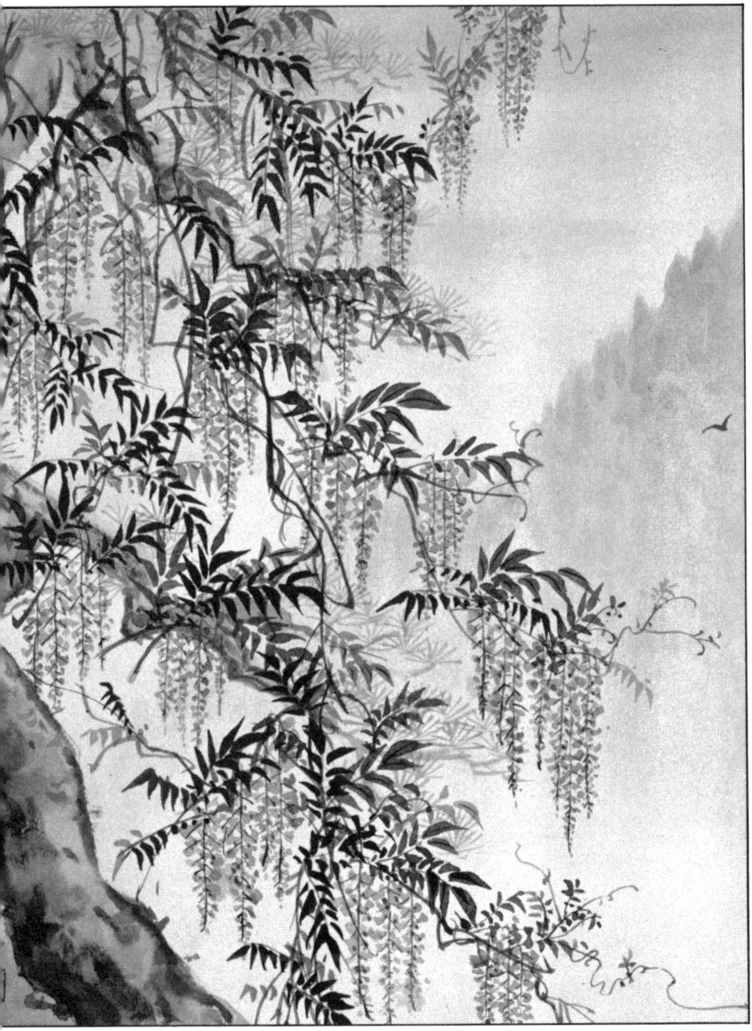

Fifteen monks sitting
almost hidden in shadows—
black robes, white faces.

A temple garden—
    green blades pulled up from the sand
      wither in small heaps.

The ceremony finished
    the place is silent except
    for a boy sweeping.

The open window
    lets in a smell of wet leaves.
      How soft the damp air.

Bamboo and maple
    twigs bend down at our windows.
    The weight of thin rain.

Clouds on Daimonji—
in quiet contemplation
watching them drift in.

Weighted down with rain
even tips of cedar twigs
lean toward the earth.

Each time he throws bread
to pigeons he leaps upward,
the lively old man.

Just over our roof
another bird is flying
through the wet morning.

A white peony
wide open in the sunlight.
No sound comes from it.

Within its redness
the peony has hidden
the scent of itself.

Now the path is white
    with fallen styrax blossoms.
        We climb steps of rocks.

Below, Ohara,
    but we can scarcely see it
    looking through the rain.

The same as before
    a language or a people—
        these quiet mountains.

Swimming in the air
    like minnows, leaves of bamboo—
    leaf not touching leaf.

Small spots of purple
on the path—but where above
wisteria vines?

Smell of a badger,
    sounds of frogs by a small stream.
        Pink weigela blooms.

A kingfisher comes
    to sit close by my window.
        That blue in sunlight!

Monkeys are touching
    the reflection of the moon,
        paws wet and shining.

Hakuyu's cave
    of a Taoist hermit's life
    was just here somewhere.

If we do not know,
and have never once seen it,
how can we find it?

Just a thousand days,
    or just a thousand more years—
        just that, nothing more.

Sitting quietly
    looking out on the bamboos,
nothing on my mind.

This blankness of mind—
    how restful it is to rest
        with the sun shining.

A crow and a hawk
    descending from the vast sky—
        the Kamo River.

The dogs keep barking
at the hideout of the cats
in the bamboo grove.

How strong they appear,
    white lilies just now opened
        in morning sunlight.

Brittle bamboo leaves
    falling onto my white hair
    and the red peony.

Back home in Kyoto
    again I look down the well.
        My face is still there.

The soft-hazed full moon—
    not like autumn, nor like summer,
    nor winter—shining!

JUNE

六月

*Purples and blues of
hydrangeas glimpsed amid
thickness of green.*

June/61

Just before each rain
hear the frog who lives alone
in the small garden.

After the rainstorm
    a half moon and two clear stars
        in a small puddle.

From the bridge above
    the stream of purple iris,
    how clear the water!

One white butterfly
    goes from purple to purple.
        The iris garden.

Walking across moss,
    the wood dove bows for pecking
    then continues on.

Bent but not breaking,
the trees of the bamboo grove.
A strange wind blowing.

Not concerned with fads,
doing as one likes to do.
This forest dwelling.

To live a long time
we work at doing little
and look at the trees.

His Japanese flute—
a dove looks in the window
while the old man plays.

Knowing life will end,
blueness of hydrangeas.
I am satisfied.

Alone by a path,
a pair of abandoned cats
sitting nose to nose.

Two white butterflies
    over deep purple orchids.
        The dog's chain is short.

The caged *uguisu*
    vibrates his miniature throat.
    A whole forest's song!

In the golden heart
    of each white water lily
        is there a Buddha?

All the small mountains
    swollen up big with greenness,
white mists in hollows.

Resting in the mist
and looking toward other peaks
I can see nothing!

White mist caught in trees,
    bird voices dripping with rain.
        The daylight is green.

As he strikes the bell
    the old man declares his heart
    feel only clearness.

Upon the green pond
    reflections of the green hills.
        White herons in pines!

While he eats his lunch,
    watching the black butterfly
    perched on his packsack.

An inchworm crosses
the blue packsack while we eat.
How green the slopes are!

Ants running quickly,
    the mealy bugs go slowly,
        over the wet moss.

What are you seeking,
    O wood dove in the bamboos?
    Summer's first beetles?

Planting the rice shoots—
    heads bent down toward the water,
        blue sky at their feet.

Inside a field's walls
    thousand of purple thistles.
    No one has seen them.

The splendid old man,
already one with his God,
yawns, laughs, belches, coughs!

On the narrow path
    of rice-field ponds, startled frogs
        leap in as we step.

Spirit well nourished
    while eating water and mist
    on this lonely peak.

With the pleasant breeze
    pairs of pine needles sometimes
        drift inside the room.

The old Buson book
    has chewed-out pathways of worms
    like calligraphy.

JULY

七月

*What sounds as a frog
rising up through the water
mounts a lily pad?*

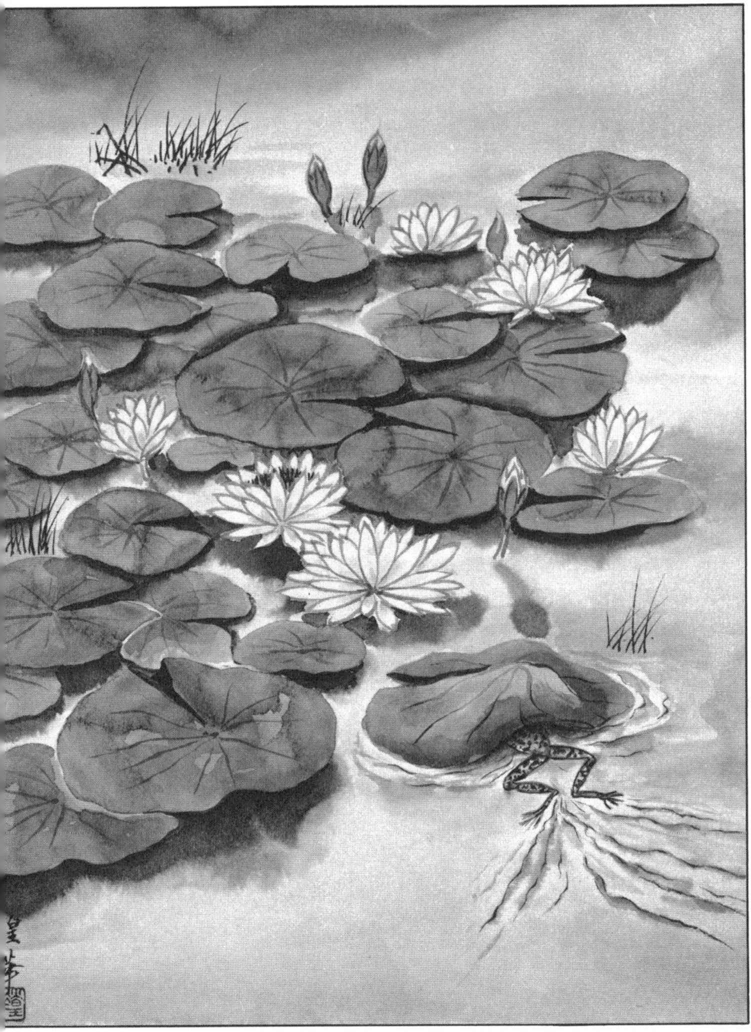

Living in leisure
at the foot of Mount Hiei,
white sand in the stream.

Water on the walls,
    insects in every room—
        this mountain cottage.

The fly on the screen
    does not really want to enter,
    but there he buzzes.

Before we were born
    and after we go are not
        the old man's concern.

Have the rains ended?
    This sunset sky has brightness
    and a cat is calling.

Feathers on the moat,
wind moving water surface
like wrinkled silk.

Three images—
    swan, reflection, shadow.
        The quiet pond.

Playful tortoises
    inside the emperor's pond
    stop to touch noses.

My eyes and your eyes
    both looking at the forest.
        Rain on our window!

Even a cockroach
    desperate to continue!
    Dragging broken feet.

Waking up I see
a new moon in the pines
and an empty room.

As white as thin clouds
    the daylight moon is riding
        through blue summer sky.

Young ferns growing out
    from bare rock and the rock cliff
    slowly breaking down.

This year not climbing
    but at least hiking past it—
        the gigantic rock!

Just one drop of dew
    reflects the whole sun's burning.
    Ten millions of leaves.

Poled upstream between
the mountains of the monkeys.
Coolness on water!

Without attachments,
    floating through the universe,
        would it be lonely?

Listless tied-up dog—
    tail wagging, leaping about?
    A beetle walks by.

"*Mu-shi, mu-shi, mu!*"
    This cricket too getting
        his nirvana.

"Hu-sh, hu-sh, hush!"
    Wind and trees with one voice
    chanting their mantra.

Just a single crow
at the summer day's ending
crossing the white moon.

Some cliffs straight up,
    some cliffs straight down, neither
        can be our route.

Lost on the mountain
    just one ridge from the city,
    yet completely lost.

Steep slopes and great trees
    in soft rain: birds and a bell.
        There is nothing else.

Running from the moon
    he falls face down upon it
    crossing a small stream.

Looking at mountains
from the top of a mountain
there is no city.

Lush pines and clear springs
    rise up from the mountainside
        where the pathway is.

Walking with the trees,
    flowing water, and mountains;
    mind empties and fills.

On a mountain path
    being dragged away by ants,
        a writhing worm.

We walk easily
    because the path goes downward
    through pines and cedars.

AUGUST

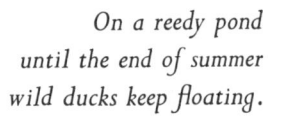

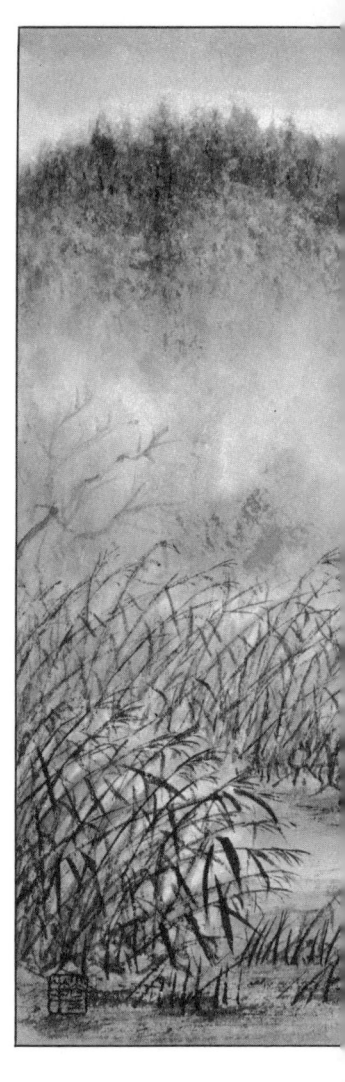

八月

*On a reedy pond
until the end of summer
wild ducks keep floating.*

August / 77

Because our dwelling
lies next to a mountain stream
and bamboos—happy!

As they wither up
    they fill the room with fragrance—
        cut-off cedar twigs.

The dogs not barking
    as we grope past the gateway
    coming home at night.

One day—two inches—
    morning glory climbing up
        to a place to bloom.

In a green garden
    a white cat going slowly
    sniffs at wet grass-blades.

This gentian flower
in the midst of blue gentians
opens its coolness.

Asked about gentians,
    the happy old man says, "Saaa—."
      Then, "Very lovely!"

Mind like a blue sky
    the happy old man always
    lives without hindrance.

A typhoon coming!
    On the vine that climbed a tree
      yellow squash blossom.

On Maru Mountain
    tossing leaves turned inside out
    show white in the wind.

After the typhoon
green rice fields ripple in wind
like waves of a sea.

Above the river,
    their continual motion;
        swallows at sunset.

By the hermit's rocks
    moss and purple stalks of bloom.
    Typhoon winds in pines.

Tiring on the climb,
    foolish things are forgotten—
        finally nothing.

Watching the burning
    Daimonji's ritual fire,
        these crowds—purified?

The one lotus bud
on the pond, not yet open,
does not know it waits.

From orange lilies
    a black cat with cicada
        in its mouth leaps out.

Now in the garden
    lilies are almost finished
    and the wind has cooled.

Mount Hiei's white heart
    aeons after aeons
        washing down as sand.

Red sashes of priests,
    purple banners on porches.
    Chanting of insects.

On the forest path
to Dogen's grave we look down
into ferns and clouds.

A new quarter moon
    lights up the wooden doorway—
        a forest temple.

Burning piles of grass—
    along the river, smoke hides
    all of Mount Hiei.

Rice fields in the hills,
    gold terraces half-enclosed
        by slopes with pines.

With the storm the wind
    has pushed all the blown-down leaves
    to the lake's far side.

Leaves of bamboo
catch the first stirring of air
at sunset after rains.

On top of the ridge,
    hot and no streams, but a view
        of all the ridges.

The voice of a stream
    far, far below this high path—
        dimly we hear it.

We say it is still
    but rain, breezes, and crickets
        distinguishable.

Single dragonfly
    crossing the Zen garden's width.
    The locust voices.

SEPTEMBER

九月

*The tender greenness
of young* hagi *bushes
with no flowers yet.*

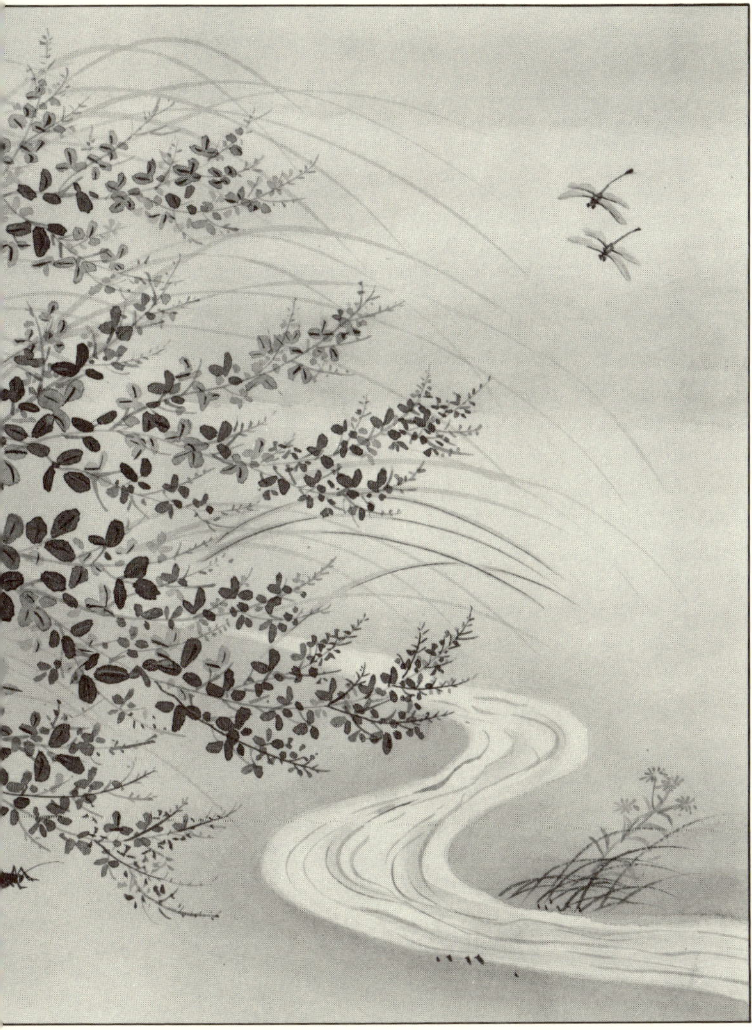

Visiting a friend,
walk through clouds and trample grasses
in pathless places.

Come hawks and circle
    overhead while I sit here
        upon this rock now.

Again this morning
    a hawk soars by the mountain
        seen from my window.

With transparent wings
    lifting the scarlet body,
        the first dragonfly.

The dragonfly too
    as it rides upon your hat,
        all vivid scarlet!

Tawny fields of rice
edged by rows of red lilies
and quick dragonflies.

Red autumn lily
    in sand by the temple step.
        Will someone take it?

Cutting down the rice.
    In air over golden fields
    swarms of dragonflies.

Stretching in the warmth,
    young dog almost smiles at me.
        Strong morning sunshine.

Small chrysanthemums
    just beyond a broken gate,
    though no one lives there.

Now a black cat darts
from under dripping hedges
and slaps at wet leaves.

Before the typhoon
    we try to speak just kindly
        in the sultry air.

How many typhoons
    did Hakuyu sit through here,
    not at all disturbed?

Before the typhoon
    a mourning dove is perched on
        the high antennae.

In the thunderstorm
    a gardener's truck heaped with
    cut-off cedar twigs.

Carrying a tree,
the woodcutter going home
treads down the mountain.

On this mountain too,
    gentians touched by shifting clouds.
      How blue their centers.

Nothing but wide sky
    and a small cluster of leaves
    with wide blue gentians.

Clouds coming lower
    down the slopes conceal our paths.
      Looking up, nothing!

Does he feel something,
    the insect ending his life
    while legs wave in air?

Dripping of the tap
brings back sounds of the small streams.
Kneeling to drink there.

Just a vague feeling
remains of my night of dreams.
My whole life also?

Very dark outside.
Coming inside the bedroom,
voices of crickets.

Between the bamboos
sunset changes to darkness.
Cricket songs begin.

Voices of crickets.
A full moon and one large star.
The first cold evening.

Now the dappled clouds
screening the stars and the moon
appear and vanish.

In this bright moonlight
    the black wall of the mountains
        looks like one long shape.

Because it has cooled
    the night will be good for sleep.
    Crickets are awake.

Time to go to sleep
    while the moon shines on and on
        lighting up my bed.

We do not see them,
    but even fallen asleep
    we know the crickets.

OCTOBER

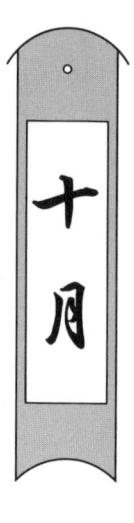

十月

> *Here a hundred times,*
> *Basho and Buson's tea hut.*
> *Now, autumn sunshine.*

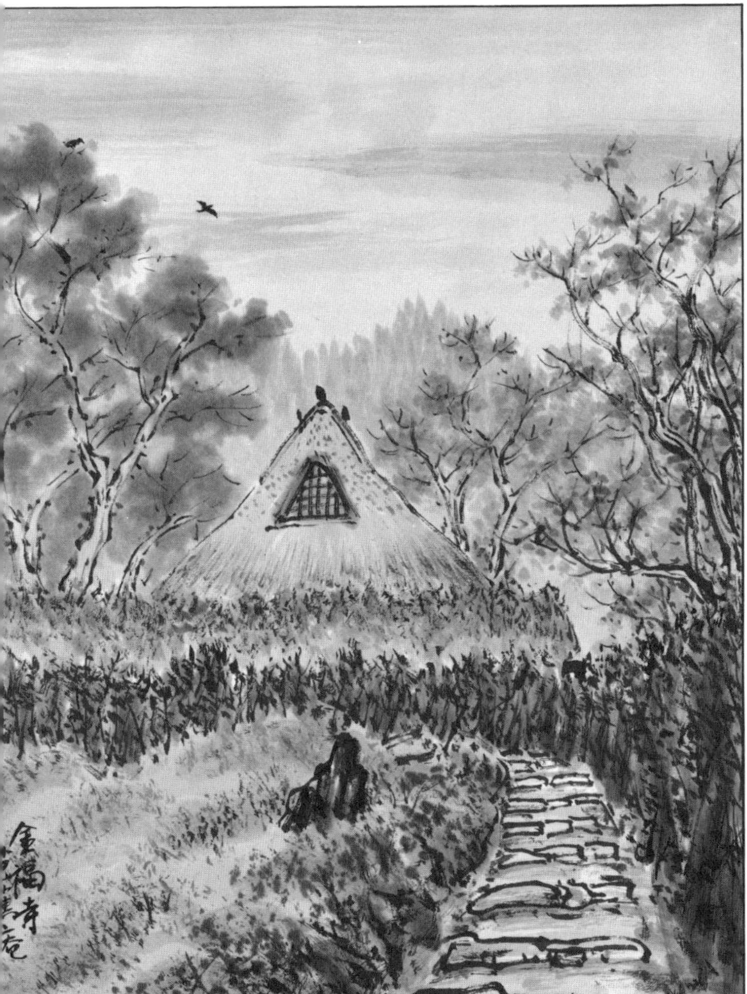
金福寺

Having glimpsed its mind
I no longer want to kill
that same old cockroach.

We walk quietly
    where only the trees can stay
        rooted on steep slopes.

Pushing back red leaves
    to look at the waterfall
        I have been hearing!

Just the water sounds
    as it descends on boulders
        fallen from ridges.

Never at nighttime
    humans staying in this place,
    just cedars and cliffs.

Reeds at the pond's edge,
seeing and hearing them move.
Four crows fly over.

A faint splashing sound
   from the ducks on the pond—
      flapping wings and diving.

Cut rice hung to dry
   on shorn ground, uncut fields still
   gold between green hills.

On the rusty rail
   of a narrow footbridge
      dragonflies resting.

Heron on a rock
   inside the Kamo River
   watching for a fish.

The herons are white
by autumn leaves on the hill.
Sky and pond are blue.

Watch the white heron
    back and forth over the pond
        silently floating.

Nothing and a cat
    inside an old Zen garden—
        foggy autumn noon.

Why do *hiyo* birds
    sound so quarrelsome today?
        Are persimmons ripe?

Just one cloud floats by
    suddenly bringing a chill—
        the south balcony.

For whom do they chant
all night, the crickets like monks,
tenor and baritone?

Dripping sounds of rain
    blend with the voices of crickets,
        the night dark and chilled.

Awake all night
    thinking I might be dying—
    the sweet-voiced crickets.

The sky this morning
    completely empty and bright
        from a week of rain.

A week of dark clouds
    and now this clear blue sky.
    Dogs stretched out, at ease.

Mountain crows come down
to make a noise in the pines—
old temple garden.

From a pruned-back tree,
    watching eight lanes of traffic,
        a crow leans downward.

A gap in the hedge—
    a thatched roof and the top of
    one persimmon tree.

Bamboos the same height—
    through the fencework of their stems
        sunrays emerging.

Underneath the trees
    golden drifts of ginkgo leaves.
    Must we step on them?

Tops of the trees bare
but underneath the ginkgos
the road is golden.

Leaves of the ginkgo
    become pieces of sunlight.
        The sky full of clouds.

The way up the slope
    goes between rocks and water.
        A badger's footprints.

Beside Buson's grave
    a mosquito clings to my leg
        though almost winter.

Dewdrops on the moss,
    holding the autumn sunshine.
        Ferns and rocks are warmed.

NOVEMBER

十一月

> *Eating persimmons,*
> *the birds screech at each other.*
> *Silence of sunlight!*

November / 101

At Honen-in
at the time of reddened leaves
between the green leaves.

Sky full of bright leaves
and shadows on sandy paths.
The purple asters.

Day by day more red,
maples outside the window.
Eating while looking.

Brighter and brighter,
leaves by the kitchen window
along with our soup.

A cold stream flowing
through a screen of bamboo stems
and redness of leaves.

Dead, dead, dying, dead—
all the red leaves drifting down
everywhere on earth.

Looking up at maples
    we shield our eyes from sunlight,
        but the leaves, so red!

Su Tung-po's Red Cliff
    and this cliff of red maples.
        Shall we picnic here?

Seeing the autumn
    foliage year after year
        and still responsive!

That small yellow bird
    still comes to the house's eaves
        and the rain still falls.

Which house am I in?
And how old should I be now?
Waking from a nap.

Sunrise or sunset?
    As I get my eyes open,
      a colorful sky.

Watching the sunset
    while a white moon rises up,
    coldness on my face.

On the leafless trees
    orange balls of persimmons
      softer every day.

Persimmon tree roots
    shining after being swept
    like old polished bronze.

There by Buson's grave,
on top of the camphor tree
a crow is cawing.

How kindly he makes
    tea, pares apples, brings out cakes—
        the wifeless old priest!

The tiny mosses
    reach out all over the ground.
    Dried leaves scattered there.

Pine-tree branches sprawled
    like strokes of a writing brush
        over garden moss.

Gratitude for leaves
    remembered as bright landscapes
    this autumnal day!

Around and around
the penned dog whirls, tail wagging.
A red leaf blew in.

Cold and dark today.
    Young dog will not look at me,
        sulking in her house.

Too many red leaves,
    too many pink sazanquas.
Time for winter rest.

For just these few days
    leaves like flames burning the earth—
        then winter dullness.

Without any leaves
    the oak stands in the coldness
    again this winter.

Through the inn's window
Kamo River with herons
and Mount Hiei.

Five herons bowing
    to one another until
        all but one flies off.

Dozens of herons
    wading the Kamo River.
    Today's bright sunshine!

Sazanqua petals,
    each white and somewhat crinkled
        on Shisendo's sand.

By sazanqua blooms
    sensing the first mountain snow.
    Sunshine on my legs.

DECEMBER

十二月

*Oh, sparrows have come
onto our south balcony
out of the snowstorm.*

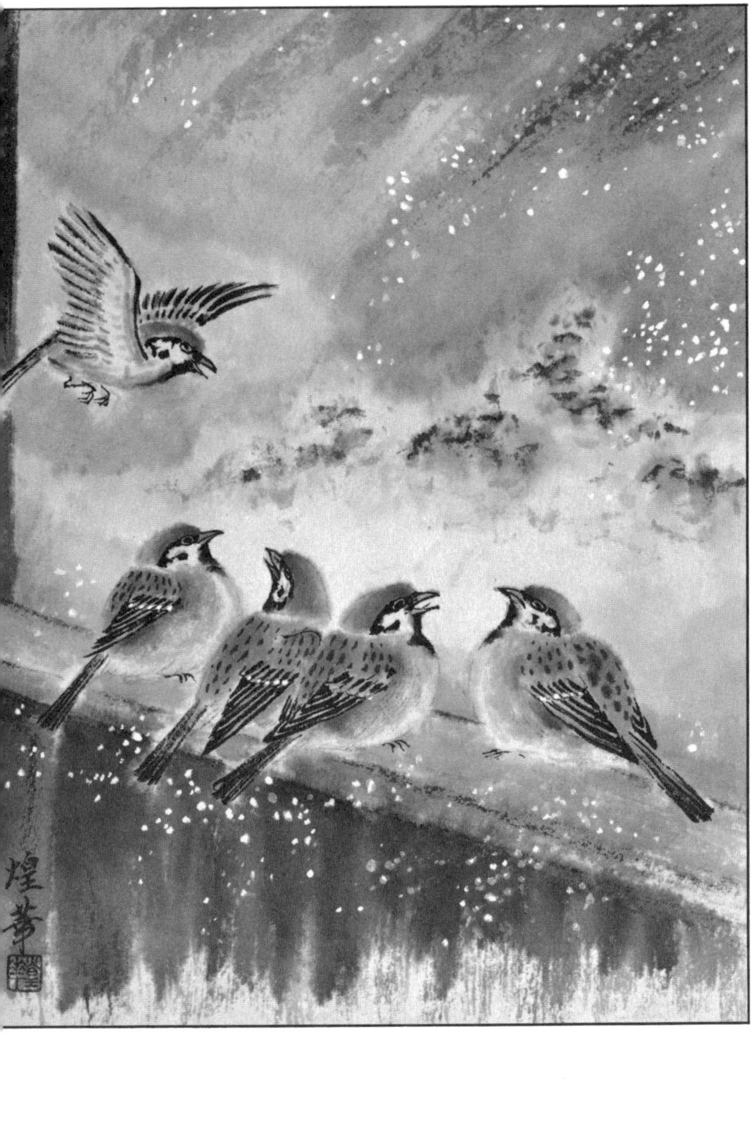

In the near mountains
perhaps it will snow tonight.
Sleeping with socks on.

Silence in the house
    and stillness of snow outside.
        The warmth of the bed.

Four electric cords
    tangled on a chair rocker.
Kyoto in winter.

Already on paths
    a renaissance of mosses.
        Another year ends.

All over the tree—
    on the ground under the tree—
    such pink sazanquas.

Along the pathway
a tree of white sazanquas
seems to be floating.

Where is Buddha mind?
    Just look at the sazanqua
        flowers in winter.

Why should anyone
    be in pursuit of the self?
    It cannot escape!

On the mountainsides
    a touch of white this morning.
    The old dog shivers.

Because it is cold
    young dog stays inside her house
    peering out the door.

The chained dog greets me
each time I pass her lonely house.
Darkness comes early.

Night after night
    we watch these same stars
        and bit by bit we age.

Entering winter—
    the gulls from Siberia
    find this sunshine warm.

Warming each other,
    thermos on my back and I—
        cold-mountain pleasures.

Spider on his web,
    green and black, as we climb up
    to Basho's hut.

Silence in the pines—
where Basho and Buson were,
just a few red leaves.

All the temple roofs
    are heavy with fallen snow.
        White and black mingle.

Lifted in the hands
    and used for washing the face,
    the cold water steams!

Silent at *zazen*,
    the rows of black robes.
        Snow blown from treetops.

The sutra chanted
    at five in the morning, steam
    from each open mouth!

At morning *zazen*
no one remembers the cold.
The whack of the stick!

By Hakuyu's cliff
    cold in the winter mountains
        we sweep the ground clean.

Resting in sunshine,
    a hundred pigeons crouching.
    Temple in winter.

A cat in the park
    crawls under dried azaleas
        when I call to it.

A hundred sparrows
    flying together somewhere
    rush by and vanish.

First snow on the roofs.
Young dog and old dog barking
to call me outside.

The carp too are cold,
    close at one end of their pond
        just before New Year.

Thick snow for an hour
    then the air is clear and cold.
    The last night came soon.

Centered in the sky
    a shining piece of the moon.
        How lovely it is!

One narcissus stalk
    gives to the end of the year
    a smell of springtime.